Asombrosos animalitos / Busy Bugs

ARAÑAS
SPIDERS

Bray Jacobson
Traducido por / Translated by Diana Osorio

Please visit our website, www.garethstevens.com. For a free color catalog of all our high-quality books, call toll free 1-800-542-2595 or fax 1-877-542-2596.

Library of Congress Cataloging-in-Publication Data
Names: Jacobson, Bray, author.
Title: Arañas / Spiders Bray Jacobson.
Description: New York : Gareth Stevens Publishing, [2022] | Series: Asombrosos animalitos / Busy Bugs | Includes index.
Identifiers: LCCN 2020008097 | ISBN 9781538269596 (library binding) | ISBN 9781538269602 (ebook)
Subjects: LCSH: Spiders–Juvenile literature.
Classification: LCC QL458.4 .J37 2022 | DDC 595.4/4–dc23
LC record available at https://lccn.loc.gov/2020008097

First Edition

Published in 2022 by
Gareth Stevens Publishing
111 East 14th Street, Suite 349
New York, NY 10003

Copyright © 2022 Gareth Stevens Publishing

Translator: Diana Osorio
Editor, Spanish: Rossana Zúñiga
Editor, English: Kristen Nelson
Designer: Katelyn E. Reynolds

Photo credits: Cover, p. 1 LionH/E+/Getty Images; p. 5 Alongkot Sumritjearapol/Moment/Getty Images; p. 7 sandra standbridge/Moment/Getty Images; p. 9 Andrea Incerti /500px/Getty Images; pp. 11, 24 (eggs) Janny2/ iStock / Getty Images Plus; p. 13 dennisvdw/ iStock / Getty Images Plus; pp. 15, 24 (shed) Astrid860/ iStock / Getty Images Plus; p. 17 Jose A. Bernat Bacete/Moment/Getty Images; p. 19 Chico Sanchez/Getty Images; pp. 21, 24 (web) Albert photo/Moment/Getty Images; p. 23 shikheigoh/ RooM/ Getty Images.

All rights reserved. No part of this book may be reproduced in any form without permission in writing from the publisher, except by a reviewer.

Printed in the United States of America

Some of the images in this book illustrate individuals who are models. The depictions do not imply actual situations or events.

CPSIA compliance information: Batch #CSGS22: For further information contact Gareth Stevens, New York, New York at 1-800-542-2595.

Contenido

Busquemos arañas 4
Un cuerpo de insecto 8
El ciclo de vida de la araña 10
Hora de comer 20
Palabras que debes aprender 24
Índice 24

Contents

Finding Spiders 4
Bug Body 8
Spider Life Cycle 10
Mealtime 20
Words to Know 24
Index. 24

Las arañas viven
en todo el mundo.

....

Spiders live all over
the world.

Pueden vivir en climas cálidos o fríos.
¡Viven en el agua!

....

They can live in warm or cold weather.
They live in water!

Tienen ocho patas.
Su cuerpo tiene dos partes.
....

They have eight legs.
They have two body parts.

Las madres ponen huevos.
¡Pueden haber cientos!

....

Mothers lay eggs.
There can be hundreds!

Los bebés parecen adultos pequeñitos.

....

Babies look like tiny adults.

A medida que crecen, mudan de piel.

....

They shed skin as they grow.

15

Las arañas viven solas.

....

Spiders live alone.

Se mueven rápido.
¡Se esconden!

....

They move fast.
They hide!

Muchas hacen telarañas.
Algunas telarañas
las ayudan a
atrapar comida.

....

Many make webs.
Some webs help
catch food.

21

Las arañas
comen insectos.
¡Algunas comen
otras arañas!

....

Spiders eat bugs.
Some eat other spiders!

Palabras que debes aprender
Words to Know

huevos / eggs   mudar de piel / shed   telaraña / web

Índice / Index

bebés / babies, 12
cuerpo / body, 8
comida / food, 20, 22